Dear Parents:

Congratulations! Your child is ta
the first steps on an exciting journey.
The destination? Independent reading!

STEP INTO READING® will help your child get there. The program offers
five steps to reading success. Each step includes fun stories and colorful
art or photographs. In addition to original fiction and books with favorite
characters, there are Step into Reading Non-Fiction Readers, Phonics Readers
and Boxed Sets, Sticker Readers, and Comic Readers—a complete literacy
program with something to interest every child.

Learning to Read, Step by Step!

Ready to Read   Preschool–Kindergarten
• big type and easy words • rhyme and rhythm • picture clues
For children who know the alphabet and are eager to
begin reading.

Reading with Help   Preschool–Grade 1
• basic vocabulary • short sentences • simple stories
For children who recognize familiar words and sound out
new words with help.

Reading on Your Own   Grades 1–3
• engaging characters • easy-to-follow plots • popular topics
For children who are ready to read on their own.

Reading Paragraphs   Grades 2–3
• challenging vocabulary • short paragraphs • exciting stories
For newly independent readers who read simple sentences
with confidence.

Ready for Chapters   Grades 2–4
• chapters • longer paragraphs • full-color art
For children who want to take the plunge into chapter books
but still like colorful pictures.

STEP INTO READING® is designed to give every child a successful
reading experience. The grade levels are only guides; children will progress
through the steps at their own speed, developing confidence in their reading.

Remember, a lifetime love of reading starts with a single step!

Step into Reading, Random House, and the Random House colophon are registered trademarks of Penguin Random House LLC.

Visit us on the Web!
StepIntoReading.com
rhcbooks.com

Educators and librarians, for a variety of teaching tools, visit us at
RHTeachersLibrarians.com

ISBN 978-0-593-64684-7 (trade) — ISBN 978-0-593-64685-4 (lib. bdg.)

Printed in the United States of America
10 9 8 7 6 5 4 3 2

nickelodeon

TALES OF THE TEENAGE MUTANT NINJA TURTLES

SAVE THE PEARL!

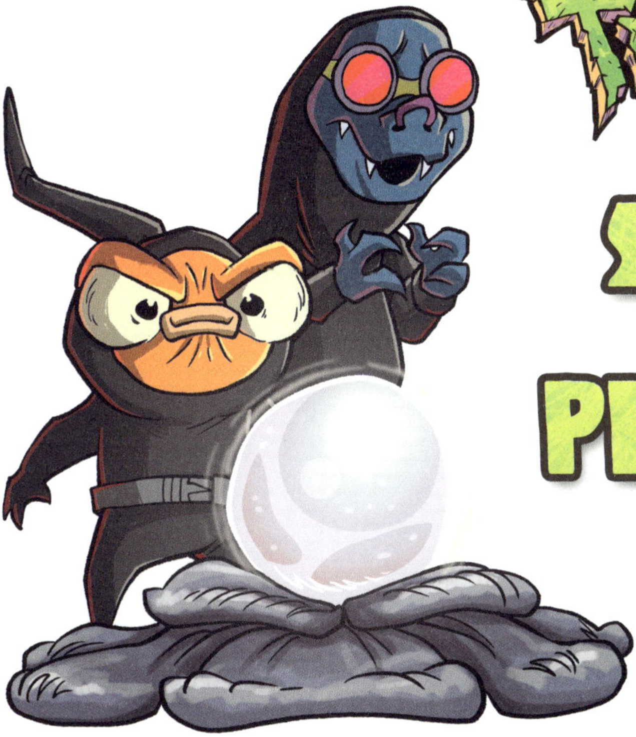

by Matt Huntley

illustrated by Nate Lovett

based on the screenplay "The Pearl" by Alex Hanson

Random House 🏠 New York

One stormy night,
the Natural History Museum
began to flood.
Mutants called
the East River Three
rose from the water.

5

Goldfin, Lee, and Mustang Sally
wanted the Jersey Bight Pearl.

Goldfin took the pearl.

Lee, a giant eel, said,

"I forgot how beautiful it is."

Sally and Lee thought
they would return the pearl
to the East River.

But Goldfin had a secret plan.
He was going to sell it
to a criminal named Bad Bernie.

Raph and Donnie were
in the sewers with other mutants.
They were chasing
the East River Three.

Instead, they found a bomb!
If it blew up,
the city could flood.

Donnie thought the bomb

was just a distraction

from the robbery.

"You two go after the river mutants,"
Wingnut said.

She and the other Mutanimals
tried to defuse the bomb.

Donnie and Raph raced to
the Natural History Museum.
Leo, Mikey, Pigeon Pete,
and Genghis Frog
were already there.

The East River Three
tried to sneak away
with the big pearl.

The Turtles jumped
into action.

Mikey took the pearl.
Then Sally grabbed it back.

Sally threw the pearl to Lee, who unleashed an electric blast from her tail.

The Turtles were shocked!

Goldfin hurled his
fin blades.
Then he ran away
with the pearl.

The blades hit a column,

cracking it.

Pieces of the museum

fell on Lee!

Sally rushed to protect her.

Goldfin escaped with
the pearl.
Now the mutants must *all*
work together.

The Mutanimals helped
Sally and Lee.
The Turtles chased Goldfin.

Goldfin brought the pearl
to Bad Bernie on his boat.
Suddenly rats swarmed
the deck.

The rats were guided

by Splinter.

He and April O'Neil

wanted the pearl back.

The Turtles arrived with the
Mutanimals.
"You lied to us,"
Lee said to Goldfin.
"You betrayed us."

Goldfin said he could buy
new friends
and tried to escape.

Just then, Ray Fillet appeared.

He had the bomb

from the sewers.

Leo took the bomb.

Sally and Lee gave him

and the other Turtles

a ride.

Leo threw the bomb
onto the boat
and sank it.
Goldfin was stopped!

Bad Bernie and Goldfin escaped.

The pearl was returned

to its underwater world.

Mutant power and friendship won the day!